CREATED BY LESLIE MOSIER AND ROB CHIANE

DOUG the PUG
AND THE
KINDNESS CREW

WRITTEN BY KAREN YIN

ILLUSTRATED BY LAVANYA NAIDU

SCHOLASTIC INC.

To Azaelea Bleichner, 9/4/2007–8/19/2021
Azaelea was the first friend and recipient of support from the Doug the Pug Foundation. Sadly, she passed away after her journey with childhood cancer. She was the true embodiment of kindness and inclusivity, and we will carry her memory with us forever in everything we do. We love you, Azaelea. —Doug, LM & RC

To you, the caring reader : Random kindness is good. Conscious kindness is gold. —KY

To Kanshu, Shubee, and Nondi—my pillars through life, the kindest of hearts, and my sisters; then, now, and always. —LN

All rights reserved. Published by Scholastic Inc., *Publishers since 1920.* SCHOLASTIC and associated logos are trademarks and/or registered trademarks of Scholastic Inc.

The publisher does not have any control over and does not assume any responsibility for author or third-party websites or their content.

ISBN 978-1-338-78140-3

10 9 8 7 6 5 4 3 2 1

22 23 24 25 26

Printed in the U.S.A. 40

First printing 2022

Book design by Katie Fitch

Special thanks to Cameo Brown

Hi! I'm Doug the Pug!

I love people, pizza, and posing for pictures.
But nothing's more **pug-tacular** than ...

spreading kindness!

Being kind makes my pug hairs fly!

Me and my humans, Rob and Leslie, need to hand out these flyers around town.

But I have a secret mission of my own: to see how many
kind things I can do along the way!

Do you want to come?!
We can call ourselves the **kindness crew!** Let's go!

Kindness is waiting your turn.

Aaaah . . . The bus is the perfect place to take a nap . . .

Or to comfort someone having a bad day.

Sometimes kindness is just being there.

Next Stop: MAIN STREET!

The Kindness Crew looks for chances to be kind wherever we go.

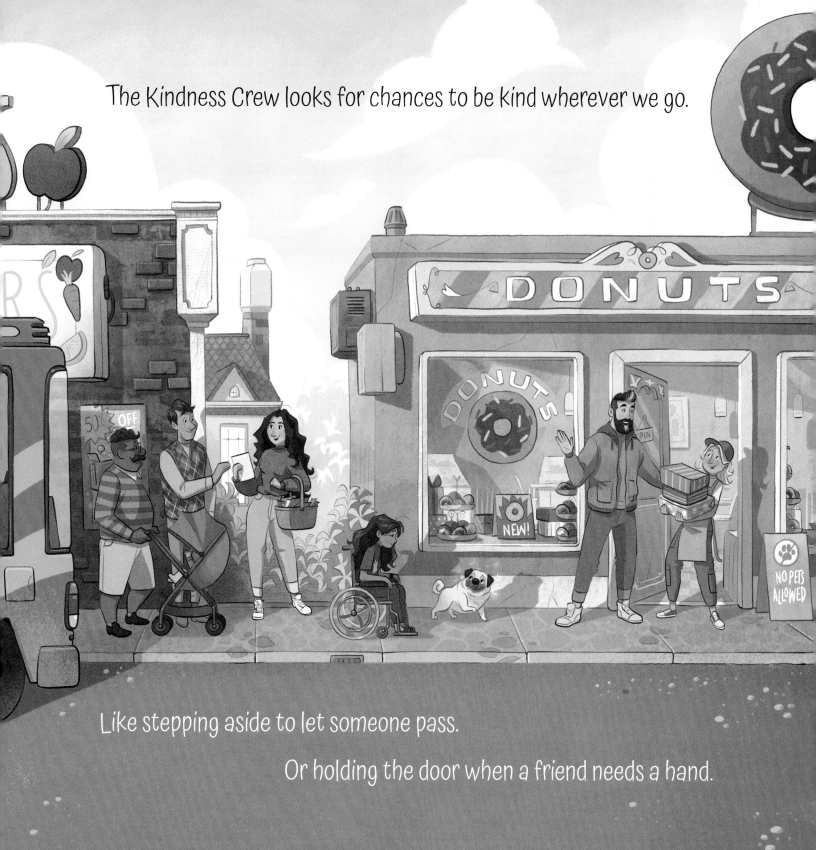

Like stepping aside to let someone pass.

Or holding the door when a friend needs a hand.

RUFF! RUFF!

Kindness is saying hi.

We all have different needs.

Some we can spot . . .

Others we can't.

So be kind to everyone
you meet!

DONUTS!

om nom nom nom!

Would you like one?

And here's one for you, too!

Kindness is sharing your snacks—
especially your favorites.

Kindness Crew to the rescue!

Even though I don't

love

heights!

Kindness is being brave for others.

Good thing the Kindness Crew loves giving!

That was close—
Hey, you dropped this!

The Kindness Crew goes out of our way to help others ...

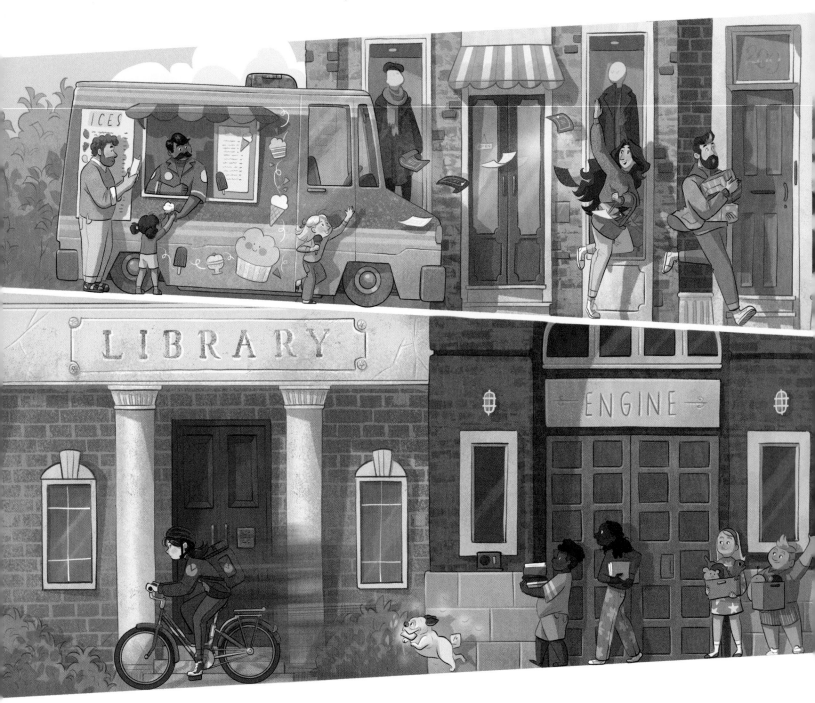

Sometimes really, *really* far out of the way.

Pizza? For me?! Thank you!

Looks like we handed out all the flyers. I'm **paws-itively** pooped. Are you tired, too?

Sometimes kindness is making time for YOU.

Unleash your inner pug and take that nap!

But not for *too* long . . .

Because it's finally time for the **PAW-TY!**

COMMUNITY DAY OF KINDNESS

EVERYONE is welcome here!

If the Kindness Crew had a motto, it would be:

"Kindness is ATTITUDE plus ACTION."

So go out there and spread kindness like pug hair . . .

(Plus, kindness makes me cuter.)

How do YOU spread kindness?

DOUG the PUG®

is a celebridog, cover model, cosplayer, actor, and the most adorable mogul ever. Doug leapt to fame in 2014 after a video of him with a pug balloon went viral on Facebook. Now, with 19 million followers across his social media channels, Doug uses his celebrity to spread joy and kindness. In 2019, the mayor of Nashville, where Doug lives, declared Doug's birthday, May 20, Doug the Pug Day. But Doug's proudest achievement is the Doug the Pug Foundation, formed in 2020, to help kids with life-threatening illnesses. Doug lives with his humans, Leslie Mosier and Rob Chianelli, and his feline siblings, Fiona and Teddy. It's true that Doug loves the smell of pizza (and posing for pictures with it!), but in real life, he dines on raw beef with steamed veggies. To find out what he's up to, follow Doug on social media at @ItsDougThePug. Visit DougThePug.com to learn about his other books.